AYE AYE CAPTAIN!

Pirates Can Be Polite

First published in 2014 by Wayland

Text copyright © Wayland 2014
Illustrations copyright © Mike Gordon

Wayland
338 Euston Road
London NW1 3BH

Wayland Australia
Level 17/207 Kent Street
Sydney, NSW 2000

Commissioning editor: Victoria Brooker
Creative design: Basement68

A catalogue record for this book is
available at the British Library.
Dewey number: 823.9'2-dc23

ISBN: 978 0 7502 8296 3
Ebook ISBN: 978 0 7502 8545 2

Printed in China

10 9 8 7 6 5 4 3 2 1

Wayland is a division of
Hachette Children's Books,
an Hachette UK company.
www.hachette.co.uk

AYE AYE CAPTAIN!

Pirates Can Be Polite

Written by
Tom Easton

Illustrated by
Mike Gordon

WAYLAND

They say good manners cost nothing but it seemed to Captain Cod that no-one had told his crew on the *Golden Duck*. That very morning, for instance, the Captain had ordered Pete to hoist the main sail.

The Captain went to see Sam, who
was busy baking biscuits in the galley.
"I'll help," the Captain said, and stirred
the biscuit mixture until his arm ached.

Sam didn't even say thank you.

Then later on, when Davy Jones walked into the captain's cabin without knocking, it was the final straw.

After all, the Captain had been in his bath!

8

"Arrr!" the Captain sighed quietly to himself.

The next morning, Nell was up in the crow's nest. She sniffed and wrinkled her nose. Something smelled rotten. Peering out into the ocean, she thought she saw a sail on the horizon. She grabbed a telescope and put it to her eye.

"Arrr!" she shouted down
to the others. "Rotten Pirates!"

The Rotten Pirates were the awfullest, rottenest, smelliest pirates on the high seas. Their ship, *The Stinky Cheese*, was mouldy and falling to bits.

Everyone was scared of the Rotten Pirates.
After all, how can you fight a pirate who
smells so terribly?

The crew didn't know what to do.
"Go and get the Captain,"
Davy Jones yelled at Pete.

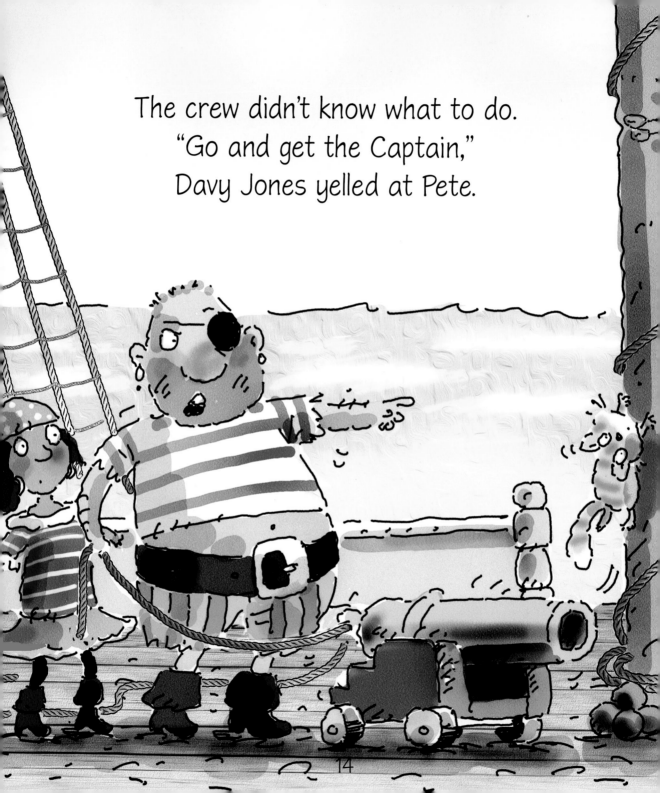

"You go and get the Captain," Pete yelled back.

Eventually Sam went, only to find the Captain's cabin door was locked.

The crew banged and shouted.
"Come out, Captain!" Nell cried.
"We need you to tell
us what to do!"

They could smell the Rotten Pirates by now.
A cloud of stinky gas rolled over the *Golden
Duck*, making them cough and splutter.
Still the Captain's door
didn't open.

"He's not listening to us," Nell said, her eyes streaming. She took off her bandanna and held it over her nose. Poor old Polly Parrot was being quietly sick into the water barrel.

"How can we make him come out?" Davy asked.

"I have an idea," Sam said, eventually.
He banged on the door one more time.
"Captain, will you come out and help us,"
he called, "...PLEASE!"

Suddenly the door opened.
"Of course I will," the Captain said cheerily.

"But what can we do?" Nell said, pointing.
"The Rotten Pirates are already beside us!"

"Fill a bucket of fresh water each, please,"
the Captain said, calmly. The pirate crew
obeyed. "Now what?" Davy asked.

"What's the one thing that the Rotten
Pirates hate more than anything?"
the Captain asked.

Sam thought for a moment.
"Bathtime?" he suggested.
"That's right," the Captain said.
He pointed to the Rotten Pirates leering
and waving their jagged cutlasses.
"It's BATHTIME!"

With that, five pirates and a parrot threw
six buckets of water right into the faces
of the Rotten Pirates who howled
and scrambled to get away.

The Stinky Cheese turned quickly
and headed for the horizon.
"From now on," the Captain said, as they
watched the rotten sails slip towards the horizon,
"if it's not too much trouble, would you mind,
possibly, being a little bit more polite, please?"

"AYE, AYE, CAPTAIN,"
everyone shouted at once.

NOTES FOR PARENTS AND TEACHERS

Pirates to the Rescue

The books in the 'Pirates to the Rescue' series are designed to help children recognise the virtues of generosity, honesty, politeness and kindness. Reading these books will show children that their actions and behaviour have a real effect on people around them, helping them to recognise what is right and wrong, and to think about what to do when faced with difficult choices.

Aye Aye Captain!

'Aye Aye, Captain!' is intended to be an engaging and enjoyable read for children aged 4-7. The book will help children recognise why politeness is important and that others shouldn't be taken for granted. It is difficult for children to learn that other people have feelings that can be hurt, and that it is important to show respect for others.

Politeness is an essential skill for children to learn so that behaving politely can become a way of life. Learning manners won't happen overnight and it is important that parents and carers don't expect too much too soon. Adults should reinforce good manners and reward children with praise.

Before reading this book, ask your child to help you write a list of what they consider to be good manners. Remember to thank your child for helping you! Then read the book together and identify what the pirates did that was rude. Ask your child when was the last time they forgot their manners. How do they think it made others feel?

Suggested follow-up activities

When the Captain is asking his crew for help, they ignore him or refuse. Ask your child whether he or she would do the same. What would your child say to the Captain if he had helped them to make biscuits? Discuss with your child why the Captain went to his cabin. How might he be feeling?

Encourage your child to be polite through positive reinforcement. Reward your child when he or she says please or thank you and ignore or deny requests that aren't couched in polite terms.

Act out the scenes in the book, perhaps dressing up in pirate clothes and displaying the relevant emotions. Then re-enact the same scenes using good manners. Discuss with your child how a few words can make such a difference to the happiness of others.

Talk about manners in different situations. How should you behave when adult visitors come to the house? How should you speak to your friends in the playground? Before entering a new social situation in which you have an expectation of particular behaviour, discuss this with your child to ensure they understand what is expected. Work together to write thank you notes after your child has received birthday gifts. If your child has difficulty with writing, then ask him or her to dictate while you write, then write their name at the bottom.

Children could be encouraged to relate an example of a time when they were polite, and another time when they were not. How did politeness/impoliteness make them feel? Has your child felt hurt when a friend or sibling was rude to them? Explain that others will feel the same way if your child is rude in turn.

Take care to be polite to your child yourself. Make pirate biscuits like Sam and the Captain and practise your pleases and thank yous as you complete each task.

Don't forget to be polite with your partner, or your child's siblings. Make a show of it. Young children watch and imitate adult behaviour. Try hard to be polite to other adults when out and about. Recognize and praise politeness whenever you see it. Children learn best through positive reinforcement. If you are not polite, it is unlikely your child will be either. A reward chart may be a good way to keep track of achievements. Add a star every time your child performs an unbidden act of politeness.

BOOKS TO SHARE

Atchoo! The Complete Guide to Good Manners
by Mij Kelly and Mary McQuillan (Hodder Children's, 2010)

This wonderfully witty rhyming story tells of the fateful day when Suzy Sue went 'ATCHOO!'. Suzy Sue sneezes but forgets to cover her mouth. The animals are astounded and decide it's time to teach her some manners.

Excuse Me: Learning About Politeness
by Brian Moses and Mike Gordon (Wayland, 2007)

This light-hearted book explores situations where children might be rude or badly-behaved. The book encourages courtesy towards others in situations such as on the bus and at mealtimes. It shows how to refuse an invitation politely, write a thank-you note and be grateful towards others.

Yucky Mucky Manners
by Sam Lloyd (Orchard, 2013)

Discover all kinds of jungle animals with mischievous manners, from burping crocodiles to unwashed warthogs. A lively manners book that shows children how NOT to behave!

Read all the books in this series:

Aye Aye Captain!: Pirates Can Be Polite
978 0 7502 8296 3

Captain Cod is fed up. His crew are rude and not very polite to him at all. When the ship is attacked by a band of Rotten Pirates, the crew don't know what to do. They rush to the Captain's cabin to ask for advice, but his door is locked and he won't answer. Will the ship be overrun with Rotten Pirates? Or could good manners save the day?

Helping Polly Parrot!: Pirates Can Be Kind
978 0 7502 8297 0

Polly Parrot loves being a pirate parrot, but sometimes life on board ship is quite hard. All the other pirates have somewhere cosy to sleep, yet nobody cares that Polly hasn't got a place to rest. Will a near disaster help the pirate crew realise that they should be more kind and thoughtful?

I Did It!: Pirates Can Be Honest
978 0 7502 8295 6

Despite being told to be careful, poor pirate Davy starts daydreaming and drops a huge cannonball right through the ship's hull. Davy is too embarrassed to tell anyone and goes to bed. The next morning, the ship is filling with water and starting to sink. Will Davy be honest enough to own up and save the ship from sinking?

Treasure Ahoy!: Pirates Can Share
978 0 7502 8298 7

Lucky pirate Sam finds a bag of gold coins buried in the sand. He hides them in his pocket and keeps his fantastic find secret from everyone else. That night, he imagines what he might spend his booty on. But then he remembers all the things that the other pirates need. Will Sam decide it's good to share?